Roly-Poly and the Light

by L. Leigh Love

Illustrated by Sonja Oldenburg

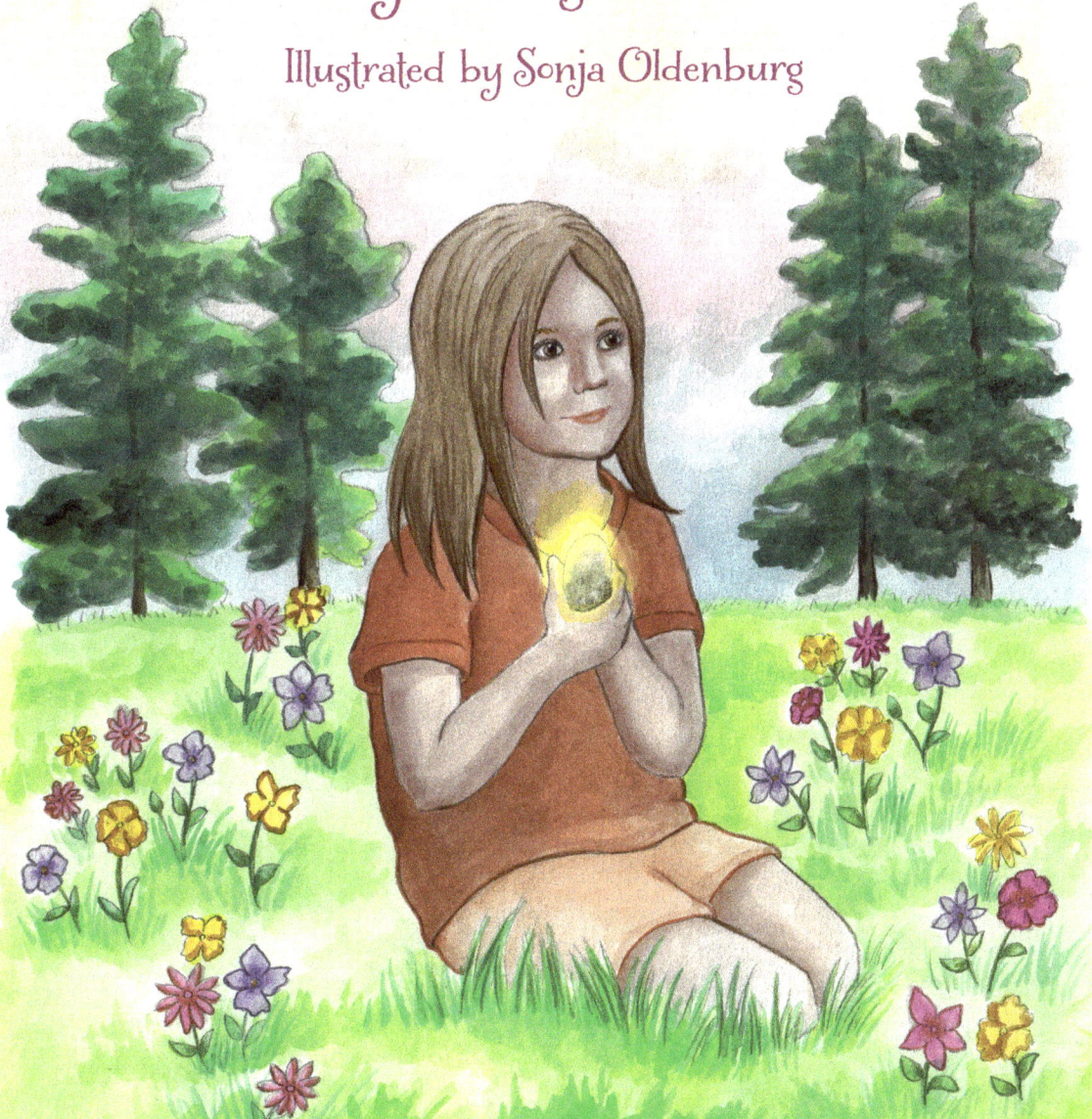

Barringer Publishing, Naples, Florida • www.BarringerPublishing.com

Illustrated by Sonja Oldenburg

Art Direction by L. Leigh Love

ISBN: 978-1-954396-09-8

Library of Congress Cataloging-in-Publication Data:
Roly-Poly and the Light / L. Leigh Love

Printed in USA

This book is dedicated to anyone who has
ever felt different, and to the
Human-Frog Alliance for Better Living.

I went outside to visit with a toad friend of mine.

I set water out for him every day. It gets hot in the summer and toads need water.

We sit and visit often, and I love our time together.

Today, he was not there yet.

I was waiting for my friend and I reached out for a stone in the water dish.

I held the stone in my hand, feeling with my heart.

It felt good to hold a piece of the earth and connect.

The stone became warm. I felt a heartbeat—mine or the stone's, I did not know.

Then I noticed a roly-poly on the ground next to me. Although, this was no ordinary roly-poly.

"Hello," I said, "What is your name?"

"Ayla," she said.

"Nice to meet you. I'm Izzie."

I had never seen a roly-poly like Ayla before and was very curious.

"You are an albino roly-poly?" I asked.

"Yes," she said.

"You are different from all of the other roly-polies?"

"Yes," she said.

This was exciting. I wanted to know more and to share.

"Sometimes, I feel different from all of the other humans," I told her.

"Yes," she said.

How wonderful she understood.

And then, I smiled because I had something in common with a roly-poly.

I sat and wondered about her life and being a part of something, yet being so different.

"All of the other roly-polies are the same," I said.

"Yes," Ayla said. "But, I am the same, too."

"How? How can you be different yet the same?" I asked my new friend.

"This is a very good question," Ayla reflected. "I will tell you. We can be both different and similar. Come walk with me and we'll explore," Ayla invited.

We strolled together down the yard to her village.

"At first, I was uncomfortable that I looked different from all of the other roly-polies," Ayla shared, "I would curl up and try to hide.

"Then I came to realize that my uniqueness is a gift. And I learned a new way of seeing myself and others.

"One night, when we were hungry, I found that with my different coloring, I could blend in and harvest food from the mushroom without being seen.

"Later, I found I was able to help lead our night travels because I am easier to see in the dark.

"It is a specialness the other roly-polies do not have.

"When I'm back home, I look around and see all of us, family and friends, working, playing, preparing meals, singing and dancing. Here, we are similar. We are living and sharing life together. And, we are all roly-polies!" Ayla continued.

"We each have our own expression of who we are. And while I am drastically unique in my expression of a roly-poly, I am still undoubtedly a roly-poly.

"Now, I look for and see how each of our differences makes us shine. Some differences are physical—some not. I love to see what those differences are.

"Also, the nice thing is that your being different does not take away from someone else being unique," Ayla said.

It really made me think.

"We all have individual gifts and a specialness about us. Each of us brings a unique part to the whole," Ayla continued.

"I'll share with you the specialness of some of my friends.

"Max has an extra set of legs and can run faster.

"Sally can't see, but can hear when the birds are near and alerts us.

"Saul knows what plants can heal our cuts, and

Abbie creates wonderful songs and dances for us.

"You are different and unique and have special talents and gifts to share. It is beautiful to know and adore these," Ayla continued.

"You put water out for your toad friend, connect to earth, and talk to me. These things you do are all wonderful, unique expressions. And your sharing these expressions helps many others.

"Being different does not take away from where you are alike with others," Ayla reminded, "Isn't that so lovely?

"To feel connected, look for what you share together."

I started to feel good.

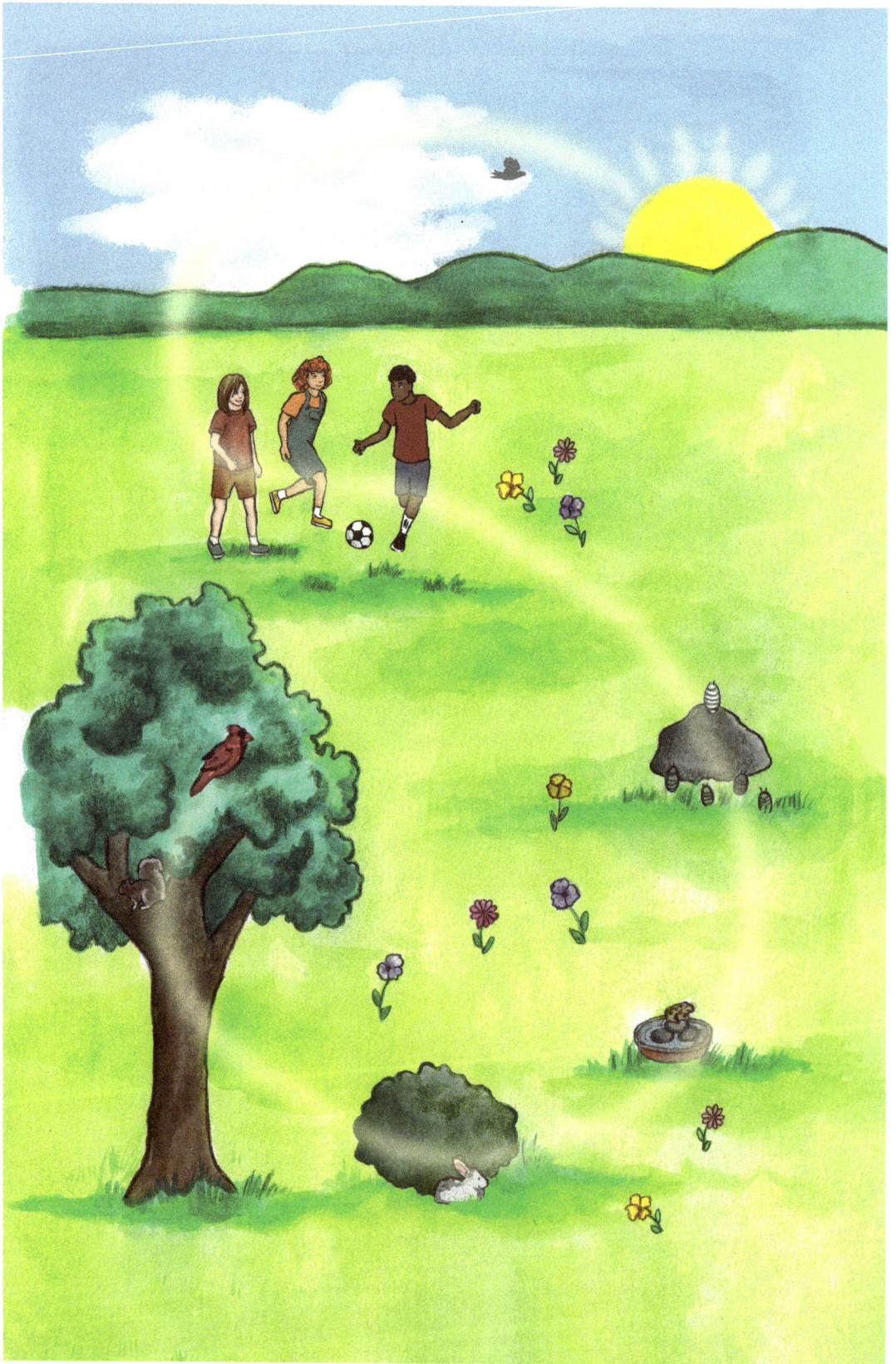

"Know that there is a common thread among you all . . . among all beings, really." Then she showed me a magical cord of light running through and connecting all of us.

"We can be both: Unique and connected . . . different and similar," Ayla said.

"Delight in uniqueness. Find similarities. Feel the joy of being you and the strength of connection."

My toad friend came to visit as we all played together.

"When you need help, just think of me and my name, Ayla."

"What do you mean?" I asked.

 "**A**dore **Y**ourself, **L**ove **A**ll—**AYLA**," she replied.

"Keep this in your heart always."

"I will," I promised to Ayla, to myself . . . and to all of my wonderful new friends.

Frogs and Toads

1 Frogs and toads are amphibians.

2 All toads are frogs. Toads are a different type of family of frogs.

3 Frogs swim and are aquatic and need to live near water.

4 Toads cannot swim, but absorb water through their skin through rain or by sitting in shallow areas of it.

5 Neither frogs or toads will give you warts. Warts on a human are caused by a virus. Warts on a frog comes from their natural glandular skin structure, helping provide camouflage and protect the skin from injury.

6 For their protection, it is best not to handle frogs or toads. Photographing them is a great way to connect.

7 Both male frogs and toads can sing . . . even underwater!

8 The world is facing an amphibian extinction crisis. Consider learning ways to support them where you live. Support wildlife conservation groups which help them.

Roly-Poly

1. Common names for Roly-Polies are Pill Bugs, Sow Bugs, Potato Bugs, Doodle Bugs, Armadillo Bugs, Cheesy Bugs, Wood Bugs, Ball Bugs, Butchy Boys, Slaters and more!

2. They roll into a ball for protection when disturbed or frightened.

3. Roly-polies are actually not bugs, they are crustaceans, similar to shrimp.

4. The roly-poly's main habitat is under mulch, fallen leaves, and rocks.

5. They play an important role in the environment by composting soil and help return nutrients.

6. They do not spread disease, bite or sting.

7. Roly-polies are most active at night.

The Human-Frog Alliance for Better Living—
is a phrase I started saying to the frogs and
toads when hanging out with them. I feel
true love and friendship with them, as with all
nature. And for fun, I will interchange species
names along the way, when with others. This
phrase embodies a philosophy of respecting
and feeling kinship with all life and a way of
being in nature, and a part of nature with
loving adoration. It symbolizes an initiative
to elevate the human, and my own, earth
stewardship. How can I, and we, be better
earth stewards and partners with life? I believe
deeply, that there are no small acts of kindness
and that every kind interaction matters.

Maintaining a water dish on the ground is a
great way to help support nature. It is often
hard for animals to find fresh water.

Many thanks to Ted Andrews for his amazing
and inspirational works with animals and
nature.

REFLECTIVE POINTS FOR THE ROLY-POLY AND THE LIGHT

1 Think about how you are different. What are your unique qualities or abilities? List 3-5.

2 What do you love or admire about yourself?

3 Think about how others around you are different. What are the qualities you admire about them?

4   What are things you share with different groups of people?

5   Think of someone who is drastically different from you. Identify one or more things you share or ways you are alike.

6   What are things you have in common with a toad? Or a roly-poly?

7   What is your favorite being in nature? What do you admire about them? What do you share with them?

8 What are ways you can support yourself with your uniqueness?

9 What are ways you can support others with their uniqueness?

Author: L. Leigh Love is an East Coast writer and artist who very much enjoys connecting with nature and all life. Her writing focuses on the inspirational and spiritual areas of life, with her artistic mediums being nature photography, acrylics, and alcohol ink. She is delighted to share the story here, which is from the heart and sparked from a real encounter with a toad friend and albino roly-poly, she once met. She also worked as the Art Director for *Roly-Poly and the Light.*

Illustrator: Sonja Oldenburg hails from Oshkosh, Wisconsin. Her work is inspired by botanical illustration, Art Nouveau, intricate motifs, and insect charts. She enjoys a lush and cluttered aesthetic, full of energy and detail in every corner of the canvas. She is passionate about drawing and illustration using colored pencils and ink pens. She loves working with an established subject and spontaneously letting it develop and grow as she draws.

CPSIA information can be obtained
at www.ICGtesting.com
Printed in the USA
BVHW012049100323
660179BV00016B/843

9 781954 396098